GRRRRR!

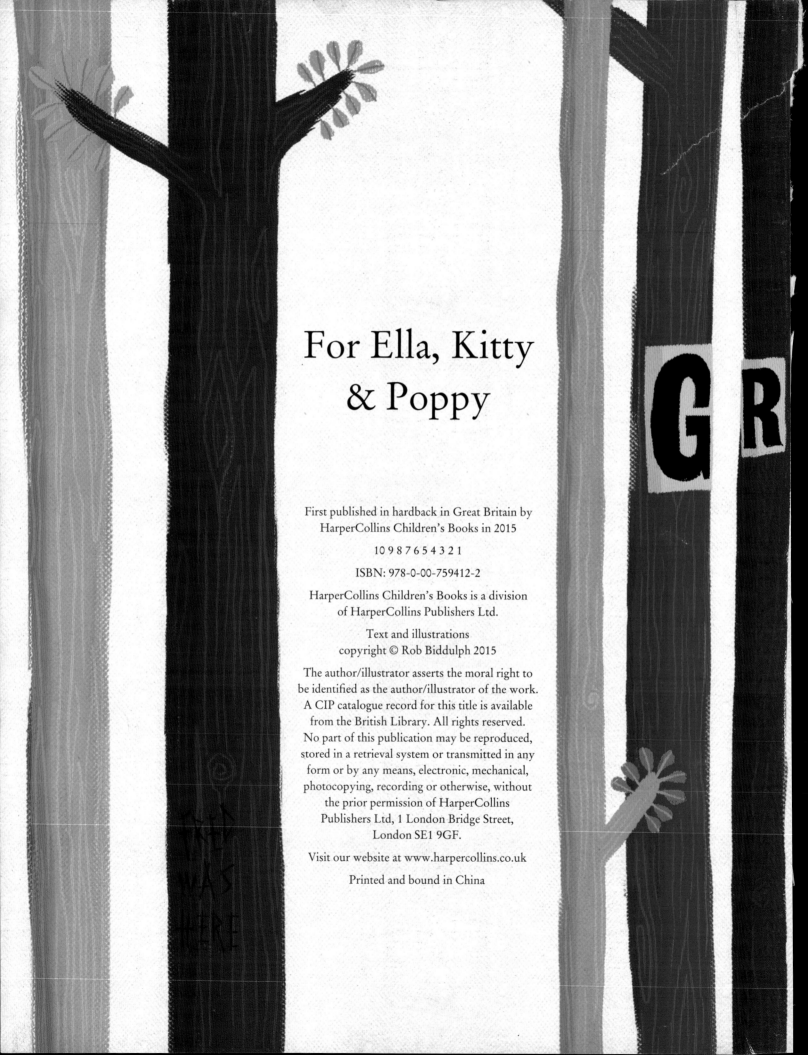

For Ella, Kitty & Poppy

First published in hardback in Great Britain by
HarperCollins Children's Books in 2015

10 9 8 7 6 5 4 3 2 1

ISBN: 978-0-00-759412-2

HarperCollins Children's Books is a division
of HarperCollins Publishers Ltd.

Text and illustrations
copyright © Rob Biddulph 2015

The author/illustrator asserts the moral right to
be identified as the author/illustrator of the work.
A CIP catalogue record for this title is available
from the British Library. All rights reserved.
No part of this publication may be reproduced,
stored in a retrieval system or transmitted in any
form or by any means, electronic, mechanical,
photocopying, recording or otherwise, without
the prior permission of HarperCollins
Publishers Ltd, 1 London Bridge Street,
London SE1 9GF.

Visit our website at www.harpercollins.co.uk

Printed and bound in China

GRRRR!

Written and illustrated by

Rob Biddulph

HarperCollins *Children's Books*

Each year, for as long as the forest has stood,
A contest is held for the bears of the wood.

And the bear that has won for three years in a row
Is a grizzly called Fred – he's the star of the show.

A brilliant Fish-catcher...

A fine Hula-hooper...

At Scaring-the-humans he's really quite super...

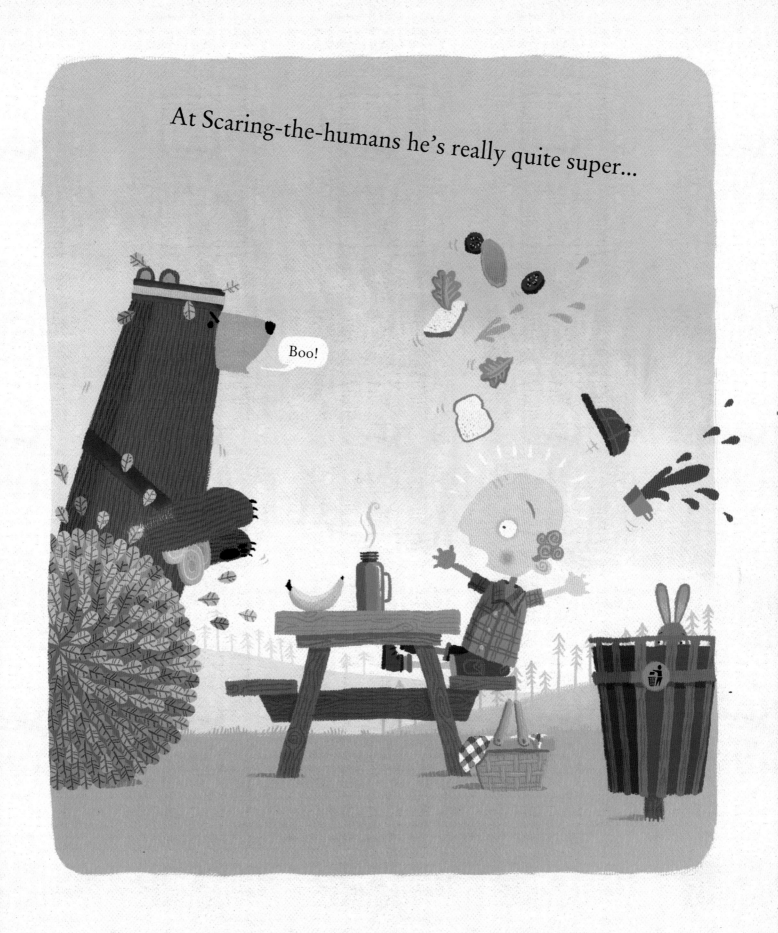

There's one thing, however, for which he's best known:

When Fred does his Loud-GRRRRR
he's out on his own.

He's on his own too,
all day long, while he's training.
There's no time for buddies,
but Fred's not complaining:

FRED

AUGUST

Now, this guy is Boris – the new bear in town.
He's entered the contest to win Fred Bear's crown.

He's big and he's strong and he's fast and he's clever.
They say that his GRRRRR is the loudest GRRRRR ever.

But why is he trying to keep out of sight,
So sneaky and quiet in the still of the night?

He's leaving Fred's cave – if you didn't know better,
You'd swear that he had something under that sweater.

The day of the contest and this could spell trouble:
Poor Fred's woken up with no GRRRRR in his bubble!

What terrible luck! What a shame! What a bore!
Two hours 'til the contest and

FRED'S LOST HIS ROAR!

Meanwhile in the treetop
a helpful young owl,
Looks down through the leaves
at the bear with no growl.

With a hoot and a flutter
he jumps from his perch.
"My name is Eugene.
Can I help with the search?"

Not sure what to do and not sure what to say,
Fred smiles at Eugene and he whispers...

"OK."

So...

They look in the greenhouse...

They look in the shed...

Then Eugene calls Hepzibah
– she soon appears.

An army of helpers all
helping our hero...

"I'm here for the hunt
and I've brought volunteers."

They look through the laundry
and under the bed...

The top of the wardrobe,
inside it, behind it...

They turn the place over,
but still they can't find it!

...But how many growls do these helpers find? Zero.

Uh-oh! Now it's time
for the contest to start…
Come along, Fred –
get a move on! Quick smart!

"Good luck!" shouts Eugene
as Fred leaves in a hurry.
"We'll all come along to
support you – don't worry!"

Best

=1=
=2=
=3=

Bear in the Wood

Start

08.58.58

First it's the Fish-catching – Fred is on fire!
Look at that score getting higher and higher!

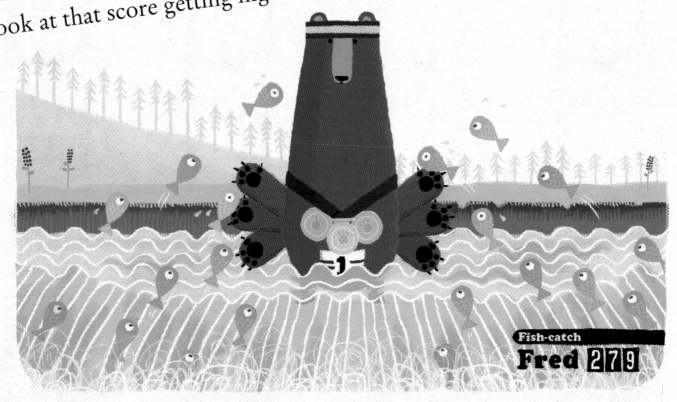

Fish-catch
Fred 279

Next, at the Hula-hoop,
Boris is spinning.
With five more than Fred
he is definitely winning!

Hula-hoop
Boris 017

At Scaring-the-humans it's hard to deny
They're both pretty scary – let's call it a tie!

Scaring-the-humans
Fred 100

Scaring-the-humans
Boris 100

And now for the Loud-GRRRRR – the last round of all.
But who's in the lead? Well, it's too close to call...

First up is Boris. A deep breath, and then...

GRRRRRRRR

RRRRR!

Look at the needle!
It's pointing to

TEN!

Now Fred's in the spotlight. He puffs out his chest.
He opens his mouth and he hopes for the best…

What an extraordinary
state of affairs!
Fred lost his GRRRRR,
but his helpers found theirs!

The sound is so loud that it makes Boris jump –
And look what just fell to the ground with a bump!

"Fred's GRRRRR!" says
Eugene. "It was you all along!
You're a bad, bad bear, Boris,
and cheating is wrong!"

GRRRRR!

"It's true," Boris cries.
"I am guilty. I did it.
I went to Fred's cave,
took his growl
and then hid it."

"I'm new here, you see,
and I live all alone.
I don't really have
any friends of my own.

"I hoped that if people
thought I was a winner,
Then maybe, sometimes,
they might pop round
for dinner."

Fred looks at Boris and what does he see?
A bear that is not all that different to he.

A bear
that is
lonely.

A bear
that is sad.

A bear that
is, maybe,
not totally...
bad.

"I think we're both winners," says Fred, "and what's more
I'd like to be friends," and he holds out a paw.

"R-really?" says Boris, who gets to his feet
And gives Fred a bear hug. Oh, isn't that sweet.

They'll always remember how this story ends:
That Fred lost his GRRRRR...

Oooh!

...but discovered his friends!